Noah Nickerson...

Snow Person Builder Extraordinaire

Written & Illustrated by Selah Hales

Printed in Hong Kong

Thank you to my family & friends who have been so supportive as I've taken on the role of illustrator/storyteller. They've been my proofreaders, critics, and cheerleaders over the past 3 years and I will be forever grateful.

Thank you Davan, for giving me the perspective of a seven year old, and for being the inspiration for Noah, from your mop of blond hair to your love of the Huskers- you're one kool kid!

Welcome readers, to the story of a little boy who learns an important lesson about doing your best....

Noah Nickerson...

Snow Person Builder Extraordinaire

In his family
the story goes
that Noah
was a
Nebraska fan
before
he was even born.

From the time his Mom and Dad brought him home from the hospital he was surrounded by what would become his favorite color:

Red...

BIG RED!

Noah was barely a year old when he went to his first game where he spoke his first words...not "mama"... not "daddy"... but on a beautiful autumn day in Memorial Stadium, as thousands of shiny red balloons floated up to the bright blue sky Noah said, very clearly...

"GO HUSKERS!"

His parents were so proud!

"Go Huskers"

Noah's house had
red shutters
and bright red flowers.

His room was red.

His bike was red.

Noah
always
wore
red.

His mom's car was red.
His dad's pick-up was...red.

Noah loved to go to games with his Mom and Dad.

He loved homecoming
week-end in Lincoln
and watching Nebraska
games on TV with
his Grandpa.

Noah liked school, camping,
roller coasters, his dog Husker,
and playing with his friends.

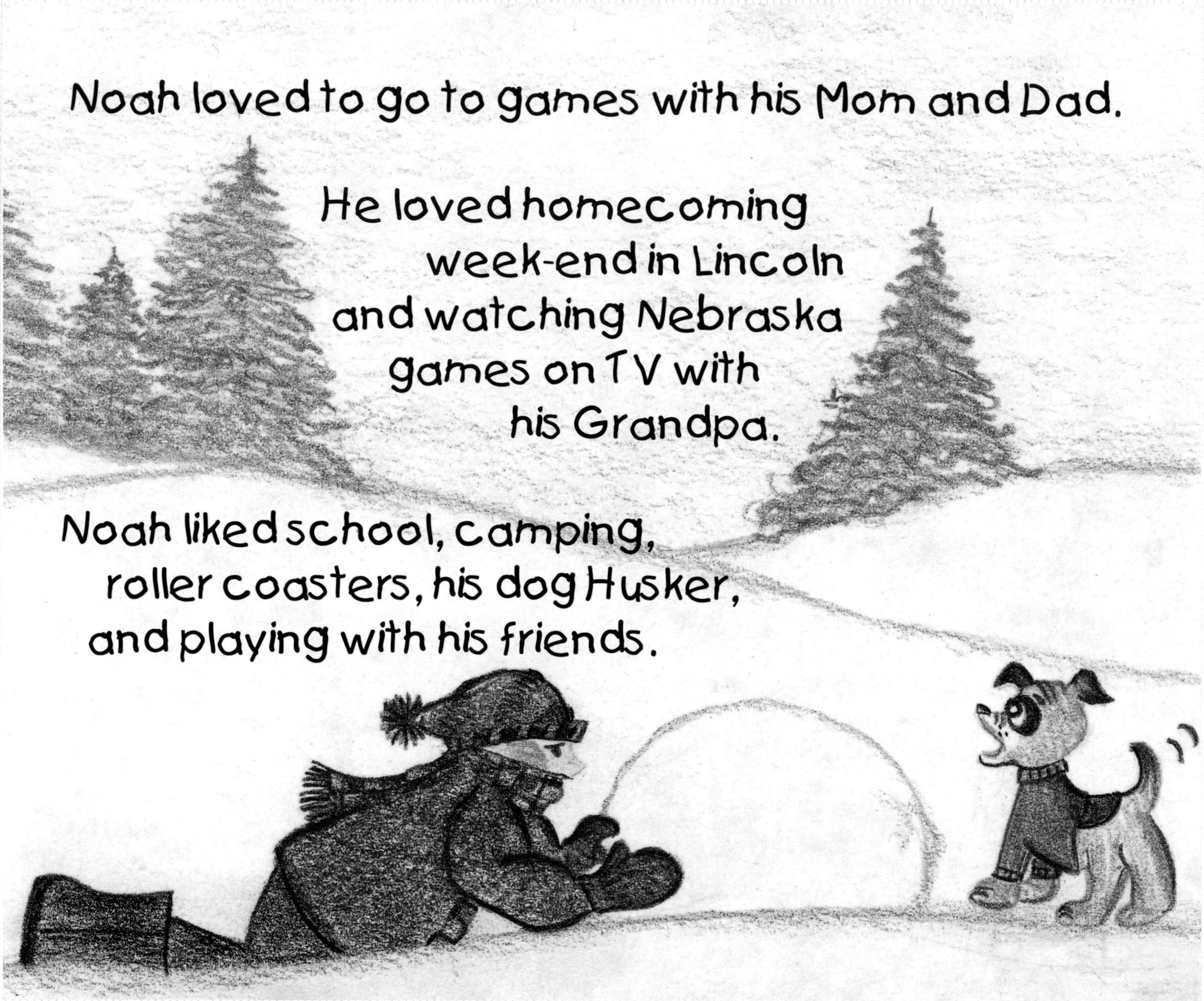

But his very most favorite thing
to do in the whole world was
building snow people
with his dad.

He would look forward to the first snow like most kids looked forward to Christmas. Sometimes the snow came in the night while he slept. Sometimes it started while he was in school. When that would happen it was everything Noah could do to concentrate on his teacher and his school work until the bell rang.

Then he would rush to get his coat and gloves and pull on his boots. Bursting out the front door of the school Noah would run to his dad's office down on Main Street. He knew his dad would be waiting, ready to take off from work to get started on their latest snow creation.

As Noah got bigger, so did his snow people. He liked to surprise his neighbors and friends with his new ideas.

The year Noah's dad used the garden hose to make an ice skating rink for Noah's snow friends they won first place in the annual Unionville Snow Person Building Contest.

They had snow people skating and sledding. His dad put a spotlight on the side of the house to light up the show. People would drive by and honk their horns or give Noah a thumbs up and yell, "Way to go!"

The next year their Nebraska Boosters Club snow people won first place again! Noah's friends and neighbors cheered him on. This was the first time anyone had won two times, back-to-back.

Noah liked winning and was already planning
the snow people he would make for the contest
the next year.

All through the summer he made his plans. Autumn came and Noah drew pictures of the snow people he and his dad would build. He had their hats, scarves and coal for their buttons in a box by the door, and a supply of carrots in the refrigerator. He was ready.

Then the unthinkable happened...
All of November and December with no snow!

When it finally came there was
barely enough to cover the grass.
Noah was outside
before the snow stopped.
Even though there
wasn't much to work
with, he was able to make
a little snowman
with dried grass and
brown leaves sticking
out all over him.

Much to his surprise, the same people who clapped and cheered when he built his snow people and won contests turned on him. "You call that a snowman?" his next door neighbor yelled over the fence, "Give up Noah, it's not worth it."

His friend Sara asked, "Why don't you just quit? Aren't you embarrassed? Why do you even bother?" Sara's brother Nick added, "Your snowman stinks!"

Noah was angry.

Who did they think they were anyway? Sure, it was easy when everyone was telling him how great he was. It was easy when there was lots of snow. It wasn't his fault that there was no snow. He did his best with what he had. He wasn't a miracle worker.

Well, if that was the way they wanted to be that was fine with him. He'd show them. Just see if he'd make any more snow people. He didn't care if there was six feet of snow. He didn't care if they begged him to make snow people. Nope, he was happy just staring at a blank TV screen. He didn't need anybody. No sirree, he was just fine.

When Noah's dad got home from work that evening, he found Noah where he had been all day.

"Your mom says your friends have been giving you a hard time. I understand that you're really angry with them. But to give up something you love to do because someone doesn't think it's good enough is wrong. We build snow people because we like to. Some years we're going to have the biggest and very best snow people in town. Some years we're going to win contests. But there will be times when we won't.

As long as we do our best and enjoy doing it, we'll always be winners. Think about it Noah, and if you decide you don't want to give up, meet me outside. I've got something to show you."

Just then, the doorbell rang. A moment later Sara and Nick were there, standing in front of Noah.

"I'm sorry, Noah. I was a jerk. True friends stick by you, even when you're not the biggest, or the fastest, or the smartest. Friends should always be there for each other. I know we hurt your feelings and I'm sorry."

"Me too," Nick said. "Your snowman didn't stink so bad, I guess. When we got home Sara and I started thinking about how dumb we were, and um... we just wanted to know if you and your dad want some help building your snow people."

“That’s okay. My dad and I make snow people because it’s fun. I like to plan them. I like to build them. If I win prizes, that’s kool. But if not, I’m not going to stop making them. Just like how I won’t stop being your friend just because you said dumb stuff about my snowman. And thanks for the offer to help. But without any snow it would be pretty hard to build any snow people...”

“What are you talking about?” asked Sara as she pulled on her coat. “You obviously haven’t looked outside lately, have you?.”

Noah opened the front door to let Sara and Nick out and was amazed to see snow. Lots of snow! While he had been lying on the couch a snow storm had covered the town in eight inches of new snow.

Sara and Nick yelled,
"SURPRISE!"

"While you were in the house being mad at us, we came over and helped your dad get started on the biggest, best snow people yet!"

There, out in his yard, surrounded by the most awesome group of snow people, was Noah's dad. "So are you really sure you don't want to make any more snow people? This is really fun, and I'd hate for you to miss it!"

Noah yanked on his snow clothes as fast as he could and ran out into the yard. "This is so great you guys. And you're right, it will be the best yet... as soon as I add my Husker fans."

So Noah got busy,
and in no time his addition to
Lovely Street's very own

HuskerNation

was complete.

Noah's dad was right. He liked it when people thought their snow people were great, but he knew being Number One wasn't everything. So Noah would keep making his snow people. He and his friends had learned that when you do something because you love it, everybody wins!

The End

Coming Soon!

Nebraska Snow People

Beautifully crafted
collectible resin figurine

Go to our website to reserve
yours today
and take advantage
of
free shipping & handling!!

Go Big RED!
Nebraska

Check out our website for:

What's New:
Books, Figurines
Fundraising Opportunities for your School or Group
Free Downloadable Coloring Pictures, Mazes, Word Searches

and more...

www.huskerkids.com

or

Contact Us...

E-mail: huskerkids@ymail.com